ABOUT THE BANK STREET READY-TO-READ SERIES

Seventy years of educational research and innovative teaching have given the Bank Street College of Education the reputation as America's most trusted name in early childhood education.

Because no two children are exactly alike in their development, we have designed the *Bank Street Ready-to-Read* series in three levels to accommodate the individual stages of reading readiness of children ages four through eight.

- *Level 1:* GETTING READY TO READ—read-alouds for children who are taking their first steps toward reading.
- *Level 2:* READING TOGETHER—for children who are just beginning to read by themselves but may need a little help.
- ○ *Level 3:* I CAN READ IT MYSELF—for children who can read independently.

Our three levels make it easy to select the books most appropriate for a child's development and enable him or her to grow with the series step by step. The *Bank Street Ready-to-Read* books also overlap and reinforce each other, further encouraging the reading process.

We feel that making reading fun and enjoyable is the single most important thing that you can do to help children become good readers. And we hope you'll be a part of Bank Street's long tradition of learning through sharing.

The Bank Street College of Education

MR. BUBBLE GUM
A Bantam Little Rooster Book
Simultaneous paper-over-board and trade paper editions/July 1989

Little Rooster is a trademark of Bantam Books,
a division of Bantam Doubleday Dell Publishing Group, Inc.

Series graphic design by Alex Jay/Studio J
Associate Editor: Randall Reich

Special thanks to James A. Levine, Betsy Gould,
Erin B. Gathrid, and Whit Stillman.

Library of Congress Cataloging-in-Publication Data
Hooks, William H.
Mr. Bubble Gum.

(Bank Street ready-to-read)
"A Byron Preiss Book."
"A Bantam little rooster book."
Summary: A boy has mixed feelings about his five-year-old
brother Eli, who sticks close to him whether he is inventing
a new soft drink or trick-or-treating on Halloween.
[1. Brothers—Fiction.] I. Meisel, Paul, ill. II. Title.
III. Title: Mister Bubble Gum. IV. Title.
PZ7.H7664Mi   1989   [E]   88-7960
ISBN 0-553-05834-7
ISBN 0-553-34694-6 (pbk.)

Published simultaneously in the United States and Canada

Bantam Books are published by Bantam Books, a division of Bantam Dou-
bleday Dell Publishing Group, Inc. Its trademark, consisting of the words
"Bantam Books" and the portrayal of a rooster, is Registered in U.S. Patent
and Trademark Office and in other countries. Marca Registrada. Bantam
Books, 666 Fifth Avenue, New York, New York 10103.

PRINTED IN THE UNITED STATES OF AMERICA

WAK 0 9 8 7 6 5 4 3 2 1

Bank Street Ready-to-Read™

Mr. Bubble Gum

by William H. Hooks
Illustrated by Paul Meisel

A Byron Preiss Book

A BANTAM LITTLE ROOSTER BOOK
NEW YORK · TORONTO · LONDON · SYDNEY · AUCKLAND

ELI

My brother Eli is five years old.
I call him Mr. Bubble Gum—
Mr. Bubble for short—because
he sticks to me like gum.
I can't get rid of him.

Mom thinks Mr. Bubble Gum is a cute name.
But Eli is a real pain.

I look after him for one hour
every afternoon while Mom works.
"Just keep an eye on him," she says.
And I say, "Very funny, Mom.
Eli sticks to me like bubble gum."

BOLO COLA

One day last summer,
my friend Roberta and I were inventing
a new soft drink.

"I hope it tastes as good as Bolo Cola," I said.
"Did you know that nobody knows
what's inside Bolo Cola?" asked Roberta.
"That's silly," I said.
"If nobody knows, how do they
keep making it?"
"Simple," answered Roberta.
"They break up the recipe.

One plant puts in the juice.

The next plant puts in a secret flavor.

Another plant adds the color.

Every plant adds a little bit to the Bolo Cola recipe. And, finally, at the last one, they add the fizz."

"Maybe we should keep our drink
a secret, too," I said.
"Okay," said Roberta.
First we mixed cherry juice
and prune juice.
It looked a lot like Bolo Cola.
"Try it," I told Roberta.

"Yuck!" said Roberta. "Too sweet!"
"All right," I said.
I added some vinegar.
That helped.
"It's flat," said Roberta.
"It needs some fizz."
"All right," I said.
I dumped in some baking soda.

Wow! How did I know that
vinegar and soda erupt like a volcano
when you mix them together?
Our new drink boiled over the pot.
It ran across the table.
It poured over the side.

And just then, Mr. Bubble's head popped out from under the table. *Splat!* He got it all over his head. Eli howled.

Mom came running.
She slipped on the wet floor
and slid right under the table!
Eli wasn't really hurt.
But the kitchen was a mess.
And was Mom mad!

If Mr. Bubble had been sticking to the television instead of sticking to me, this never would have happened. Sometimes Eli is worse than bubble gum. Sometimes he's more like Super-glue!

THE PUMPKIN HEAD

On Halloween I got stuck
with Mr. Bubble Gum again.
"Keep an eye on him," Mom said.
"And maybe you'd better keep
a hand on him, too," she added.

Eli was wearing a paper pumpkin head with the eyes, nose, and mouth cut out. The rest of his costume was an old sheet. He was a kind of pumpkin ghost, I guess.

On the first block I saw
three other pumpkin heads.
By the time Roberta joined us,
there were six pumpkin heads
running up and down the street.

"I think every little kid in town
is wearing a pumpkin head," I said.
"They were giving them away
at the Piggly Wiggly supermarket,"
said Roberta.

"What are you?" I asked Roberta.
"Don't you know Count Dracula
when you see him?"
"You could have fooled me," I said.
Roberta popped a set of fangs
into her mouth.
"How about now?" she asked.
"Now you look like you need
braces," I said.

I was wrapped from head to toe
in five rolls of white toilet paper.
It wasn't hard to guess who I was,
but I asked anyway.
"Who am I?"

"Count Dracula's best friend,
the Mummy," answered Roberta.
We laughed so hard
that Roberta lost her fangs.

"Hey, where's your bubble gum?"
asked Roberta.
I looked around.
I didn't see Eli anywhere.
Then ahead I saw three pumpkin heads.

Roberta and I ran to them.
Eli was not under any of the pumpkins.
"He can't be far," I said.
We found two more pumpkin heads.
They were both girls.

It was getting dark.
I was beginning to get angry
and a little scared, too.

Any other time Eli would be right there,
sticking to me like bubble gum
on the bottom of my shoes.
Now he was really missing.

Witches and ghosts kept running by,
yelling, "Trick or treat!"
They were having fun. Not me. I felt terrible.
It was the worst Halloween ever.
Roberta said, "Maybe we should tell
your mom."
I said, "I can't go home without Eli.
What will she think?"
Roberta said, "I think we better go tell her."

We started walking home.
I was hoping every step of the way
to see a pumpkin head,
one with Eli under it.
Once I thought someone was following us.
I looked back.
But it was only a kid with a monster mask.
We got all the way home
without seeing any more pumpkin heads.

The monster was still behind us.
I stood in front of our house,
thinking of a way to tell Mom
Eli was missing.
"Are you going in?" asked Roberta.

Suddenly, the monster pulled on my arm
and said, "Trick or treat."
"Go away!" I yelled.
He didn't.

Then something clicked.
I lifted the mask, and there was Eli,
grinning just like a pumpkin.
"Where did you get that monster mask?"
I yelled.
"Traded," said Eli.

I couldn't help myself. . . . I hugged him—
right in front of Roberta.
"You stuck to me after all," I said.
Good old Mr. Bubble Gum!

THE RESCUE

The week after Halloween,
I was going to Roberta's house.
Eli wanted to come.
I said, "No, Mr. Bubble Gum. You're
sticking somewhere else for a few hours.
Roberta and I are working on a skateboard
with a steering wheel."
Roberta said a steering wheel
would save a lot of hurt knees.

"Keep your eyes open for a wheel,"
Roberta told me.
So when I saw a wheel
right in the middle of a vacant lot,
I ran to get it.

Ouch! I fell into a hole.
My ankle hurt so much
that all I could do was
lie there and cry.

No one was on the street that day.
I lay there thinking all kinds of things.

*Maybe Roberta will come looking for me
when I don't show up.*

*Maybe a helicopter will fly over
and spot me.*

*Maybe a dog will come by
and bark until someone notices.*

*Maybe I'll just lie here until it gets dark.
Will Mom send a search party with flashlights
to look for me?*

Then I heard someone shouting.
"There! There! Over by the wheel!"
I sat up.
Mr. Bubble was pulling Mom
along the street.
He was pointing right at me.

Mr. Bubble had followed me!

Eli is getting smarter.
He isn't sticking as close
as he used to.
But he was close enough
to see me fall.
And he was sharp enough
to go for help.

That was the day I called him Eli
instead of Mr. Bubble,
when I thanked him for saving my life.